Other titles from Hodder Children's Books:

The Worm and the toffee-nosed princess

and other stories of monsters

Eva Ibbotson

illustrated by Russell ayto

Hodder Children's Books

A division of Hodder Headline Limited

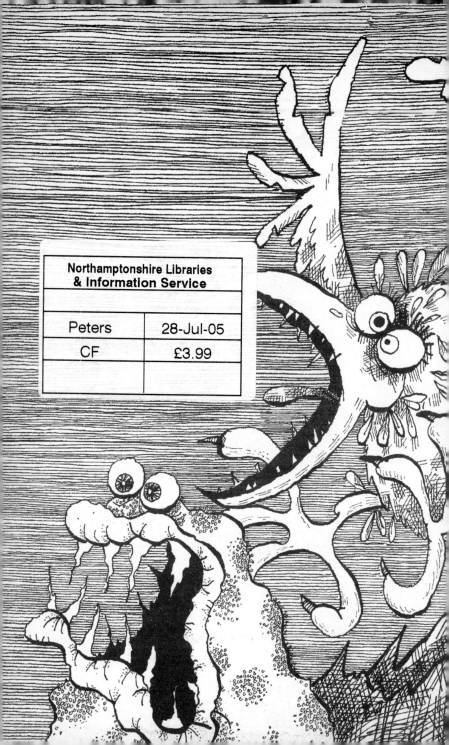

contents

the worm and
the princess who
said "phooey"

Once upon a time there lived a worm.
Not an earthworm – earthworms are
smooth and pink and soft with purple
bulges in the middle. Not a tapeworm –
tapeworms are white and flat and slippery
and like to live inside people's stomachs if
they can. Not a lugworm either –
lugworms, which people use for fishing,
stay buried in the sand.

No, this was a very different sort of
worm. It was a great, long, hairy worm
and when I say long, I mean as long as a
train or as two football pitches or as four
thousand three hundred and fifty pork

sausages laid end to end.

This worm had a forked tongue like so
many monsters and poisonous breath but
it didn't have wings; it just slithered.
Dragons have wings; worms don't. What
it did have was the power to join itself up
again when it was cut into pieces. It also
had blue eyes which is unusual in a worm.

One day this worm was lying peacefully
in a field. Its head was by the gate and
its body was looped round and round and
round the field it was in and a bit over
into the next field. And as the worm lay
there, just thinking its own thoughts, the

gate opened and a Princess walked in.

The Princess looked at the worm and the worm looked at the Princess. Then the worm lifted its head, with its cornflower-blue eyes and said:

"Good morning."

It did not say "Good morning" because it thought it was an enchanted prince and wanted the Princess to kiss it and turn it back into a prince. It said "Good morning" because it was a polite worm and that is what you say to people – and certainly to princesses – when they come through your front gate.

But the princess did not say "Good morning" back. She made a rather rude gesture and then she said:

"Phooey!"

Now "Phooey" is not a nice thing to say to a worm when it has just said "Good morning" to you. The worm was amazed. It thought it had misheard. So it lifted its

head to speak again.

"I said 'Good morning, Princess'," said the worm.

"And I," said the Princess, making an even ruder gesture, "said 'Phooey!'."

Now this worm was not particularly ferocious or troublesome, but it was a worm. Worms are like dragons or serpents: they are monsters and able to be fierce. So when the Princess said

"Phooey" to it a second time, the worm
did the only thing it could do. It shot out
its forked and poisonous tongue, wrapped
it round the Princess, pulled her into its

mouth – and swallowed her.

Then it went back to lying peacefully in the field. Well, you can imagine the fuss in the palace when it was discovered that the Princess had disappeared.

"Where is the Princess?" shouted the King, and:

"Where is my little girl?" wailed the Queen, and:

"Where is Her Royal Highness?" yelled

the servants.

Actually, the servants weren't at all sorry that the Princess had gone because she'd been a very naughty child. She'd begun as one of those babies that turn purple from screaming and kick people in the stomach, and gone on to be the sort of little girl who yells with temper if she's asked to put on a pair of plain knickers instead of lace ones. Later she was faddy about her food and snobby with the children who came to play with her and rude to servants. "Princess Toffee-Nose" they called her because that's just what she was.

But when it was discovered that the Princess had not only vanished, but had been eaten by a worm, something had to be done. So the King sent out a proclamation to say that anyone could have half the treasure in his kingdom if he would go out and slay the loathsome

monster who had devoured his daughter.
He would have offered his daughter's hand in marriage but

of course he couldn't because she had been eaten by a worm.

Then he waited for lots of princes to come flocking to the palace, but nobody came at all. This was because the Princess had been rude to so many people that no-one cared what happened to her and nobody wanted to risk being killed.

But at last he found a tired, old knight who said, "All right, I'll see what I can do."

So the Knight rode off on his rather battered old horse in his rather rusty armour to the field where the worm was still lying peacefully with his head by the gate and his body coiled round and round the field. And because the Knight was a very fearless knight he began at once to chop pieces off the worm, starting at the tail. He chopped off one piece and then another and another.

And every time he chopped off a piece he threw it as far away as he could over a hedge or into a duck pond, because he thought that if he did this the worm would not be able to join itself up again. He didn't know, you see, that he was dealing with a very clever worm.

At first the worm did not notice what was happening. This is because worms like that are so long that it takes ages for messages to get from one end to the other.

But in the end it did notice what was happening. The knight had just chopped off a rather fat and bulgy bit and was picking it up to throw it over the gate when there was a slithering, slurching kind of noise and out on to the grass fell the Princess!

She was in an awful mess! You know what the insides of squashed animals are like. Little bits of mince stuck to her all over. She was wet; she was crumpled; and she was bald, too, because the Knight had chopped so close to her head that he had cut off her hair. What's more, she was covered in bright red spots because inside

the worm she had got the measles.

Still, she was alive. So the Knight shook her out and dried her and when he had finished chopping up the worm he put her over his saddle and rode back to the palace.

The King was terribly pleased. "You brave and noble Knight," he said. "I offer you my daughter's hand in marriage."

"No thank you," said the Knight. "Your daughter is not at all the kind of person I should like to marry and anyway I am too old."

"She looks better when she's cleaned up," said the Queen.

"And when she hasn't got the measles," said the servants.

But the Knight went on shaking his head. He didn't want half the King's treasure either because it was too heavy and would tire his horse. He just took three gold pieces and rode away.

But what of the poor worm?

There it lay in the middle of the field with its sore, sad head chopped off in a pool of blood and its cornflower-blue eyes full of tears and everywhere – strewn over the hedges and haystacks and the bushes – its hacked-up pieces of body.

Slowly, bravely, all that day and the next day and the next the worm went about joining itself up and joining itself up and joining itself up. It would get three bits that fitted and then the fourth bit would roll away into the ditch and get lost and it would have to hunt everywhere to find it. Once, it had thirteen bits of tail together but the fourteenth just couldn't be found because the Knight had thrown it into a tree and some rooks had used it to hold meetings on. And the bit the Princess had been in was particularly difficult to fit on because it had got stretched and flabby at the edges.

But the worm just worked and worked and worked . . .

. . . Just before noon on the third day it finished joining itself up and then it slithered away over the fields and hills and valleys till it came to a clear, deep lake because it wanted to see what it looked like. But when it stared into the water and saw its reflection, the worm gasped with surprise.

It had made a sort of mistake. It had put its head in the middle and stretching away to either side of it, as long as half a train or one football pitch or two thousand one hundred and seventy-five pork sausages, were its two bits of body. It had a body to the right of it and a body to the left of it and in the middle was its head.

For a while the worm just stared into

the water and then a pleased and happy
smile spread over its face and its

cornflower-blue eyes danced with joy.
And it said to itself "It was a bad day
when the Princess came and said 'Phooey'
to me and I swallowed her and the Knight
chopped me up but now I am the only
worm in the whole world with a head in
the middle of my long, long body – and
thus I shall remain until the end of time!"

And thus it did.

As for the Princess, no-one ever came to
marry her – not a prince or a plumber or a
roadmender or a window cleaner – not

anyone, because if you start life by kicking people in the stomach and go on by yelling with temper if you are supposed to wear plain knickers instead of lace ones and then say "Phooey" to a worm, you are going to have a very lonely life. Which is what she did, and serve her right.

the frid
and the dog
who was silly

ostly when you climb a hill or scramble through the heather and come across a large rock it will be just what it seems: a large rock.

But sometimes – just sometimes – you might come across a rock that is not exactly what it seems. Such a rock will look strange and sinister and different.

A rock like that will be a Frid rock and inside there will be a Frid.

What a Frid looks like is very hard to say because Frids never come out of their rocks, but what they do is nasty (as you shall see).

Once there was a Frid rock on a hill above a village in which there lived about two hundred people, some cows, some chickens, some pigs – and five dogs. All the people in this village were very careful not to upset the Frid. They spoke politely and quietly when they went near the rock and they put out crumbs by it and bowls of milk because crumbs and milk are what Frids like. And the dogs were even more well-behaved than the people, because an old story said that the last time a Frid had been angered it was by a dog and though no one could remember what had happened to the dog they knew it was bad.

The five dogs in the village were friends.

There was an old English sheepdog with wise eyes, which peered out under his grey-and-white fringe of hair. There was a liver-coloured spaniel who loved everybody and wanted everybody to love her, and spent a lot of time on her back with her legs in the air so that people could stroke or scratch or even kick her if they wished. There was a Basset Hound with a body like a hairy drainpipe and ears that were full of little spiders and beetles which had climbed in as he trailed

them along the ground. There was a
poodle who had once belonged to a
travelling circus. And there was a
mongrel called Fred.

Every one of these dogs was a sensible dog. They knew that a Frid lived in the rock above their village and though they often went for walks together they took care to keep well away from the rock and if they did have to pass it, they did so quietly with their tails down. As for lifting their legs against anything within half a mile of the Frid rock, they would rather have died. Nor did the mongrel, though he was as tough as they came, ever make any jokes about a Fred not being afraid of a Frid because he knew that anyone who was not scared of a Frid was, quite simply, a fool.

And for many years the people and the dogs in the village lived in peace with the Frid and the Frid lived in peace with them, taking his crumbs and his milk at night and bothering no-one.

Then one day a completely new dog arrived in the village. She came in a

carriage with a rich and important lady
who was staying at the inn and her name
was Winsome Wilhelmina III of
Bossybank Snootersloop, from which you
will see that she was a pedigree dog and
very, very grand. She had hair on her
back which flowed down to the ground
on either side. She had hair on her legs
and hair rippling along her tail and hair on
her head, where it was gathered into a
topknot and tied with a pink satin ribbon.

When Winsome Wilhemina walked, (which wasn't very often because she preferred to be carried) she looked like a blonde wig on castors and all you could see apart from her hair were her snappy black eyes and her snooty black nose and, of course, her ribbon.

The other dogs saw her come and saw her carried into the inn, but they did not expect to see her again. She was obviously not the kind of dog who would mix with ordinary dogs like themselves. But it is no good being terribly grand and pure-bred and important if there is no one to see how grand and pure-bred and important you are and on the third day of her visit, Winsome Wilhemina trotted out of the back door of the inn, found the five dogs lying in a batch of shade under a tree – and began at once to boast.

"I," she said, "am Winsome Wilhemina. My pedigree goes back for nine hundred

years. I sleep in a basket lined with white satin and it takes my mistress's maid an hour to comb my hair.

"Goodness!" said the sheepdog.

"I only eat the best steak cut into finger-thin slices, and peeled grapes for my bowels, " Winsome went on.

The other dogs had never seen grapes, let alone peeled grapes, but they were very impressed and the spaniel grovelled in the dust and licked Winsome Wilhemina's toes.

"There are real diamonds in my collar," the little show-off continued.

"You may look."

So the dogs peered at Winsome's neck and sure enough, buried in deep in her silky, golden hair, was the sparkle of jewels.

By now the village dogs were quite overcome by the grandness of this newcomer. But Fred, the mongrel, plucked up his courage and said:

"Like to go for a walk with us Win?"

Winsome Wilhemina tossed her head. "I'd prefer you to use my full name if you don't mind. But I don't mind going for a walk as long as there's no mud or dust to get in my hair."

So they took Winsome Wilhemina for a walk.

Because they did not want her to get her beautiful coat muddy they did not take her for their usual walk along the river where there were water rats to be chased, and because they did not want her to get dried leaves in her long, silky hair they did not take her into the wood where there were pigeons to be terrified and holes to dig. Instead, they took her up the clean, straight, sandy path that led towards the Rock of the Frid.

As they got closer, the village dogs got quieter and quieter but Winsome Wilhemina didn't.

"What on earth is that absolutely extraordinary rock?" she said in her high, upper-class-dog voice.

"It's the Frid rock," said the sheepdog.

"It's best to be quiet when we go past it," said the basset hound.

"Quiet?" yapped Winsome piercingly. "Why should I be quiet because of some perfectly ridiculous rock! I've never even heard of a Frid. I don't believe there is such a thing!"

"There is, Winsome," said the sheepdog seriously. "There really is such a thing as a Frid and it's inside that rock."

"How do you know?" said Winsome, tossing her topknot.

"We know," said the poodle, "because of what it does. Especially to dogs."

"Pooh!" said Winsome. "Country dogs are always full of silly fancies."

She trotted on her stiff little legs right up to the base of the rock and began to snuffle at the crumbs the villagers had left. Then she shot out her little pink tongue and one by one she gobbled them up!

The spaniel whimpered
with terror.

"Come away,"
barked the
mongrel. "For
heaven's sake,
Winsome, come
away before it is
too late!"

Winsome Wilhemina took not the slightest
notice. Snuffling her way further along
the rock she found a saucer of fresh milk.

"No!" yelped the basset hound, "not the
Frid's milk! No, no, no!"

Winsome didn't even bother to turn
round. Out came her greedy little tongue
again and lap, lap, lap she went until
every single drop of milk was gone.

And then – you will find this almost
impossible to believe – she went and

made a puddle beside the Rock of the Frid
itself!

With a howl of terror, the other dogs
fled. A frightful silence fell. The sky
darkened; the earth trembled. And on the
face of the Frid of the Rock there
appeared something so awful that no-one
could give it a name. An eye – yet like no
eye that has ever been seen. With a crack
the rock split to form a mouth, a

bottomless hole, a something that gaped
and beckoned.

"SCROOMPH!" said the Frid.
"SQWILLOP!"

And as it said these dreadful words,

Winsome was lifted and bodily sucked,
slowly, into the hole.

The hole closed. The eye vanished, and Winsome Wilhemina had gone.

It was a long while before the whimpering dogs dared to crawl back again. But bravely they came and patiently they waited. They waited and they waited and then the awful eye appeared and the hole gaped open.

"GERTCH!" said the Frid "PFOO! BWERK!"

And on the ground it spat – a thing.

Only what could it be? It was the size of a very small rat. It was quite raw and pink and totally naked. And as it lay there, like something on a butcher's slab, it seemed more dead than alive.

The Frid had closed up again. Slowly the dogs crawled forward and the spaniel began to lick the pitiful thing with her loving tongue.

"Good heavens!" said the sheepdog, when he could trust himself to speak

again." Look – it's here! It's Winsome! She's still wearing her collar."

It was true. On the scalped, raw little rat of an animal, the collar of diamonds still twinkled.

And in that moment, the wise old sheepdog recalled what his great grandmother had told him years and years before.

"I remember now," he said, "what a Frid is. A Frid is a thing that turns dogs hairless."

And the other dogs nodded, for it was coming back to them, too, that if there is a something that turns dogs hairless then that something is a Frid.

So they dragged the poor, silly hairless little creature down to the village and since her rich mistress wanted nothing to do with her now she was so ugly, the dogs themselves licked and loved her back to health. Winsome Wilhemina became quite a nice dog, but her hair never grew again, not so much as a single eyelash or a whisker. Nor could she ever speak about what had happened when she was inside the Frid. "Let sleeping Frids lie, my dears," was all she would say when visiting dogs came and asked her questions. "That's all we dogs can do, just let them lie."

And I am happy to say they did.

the kraken
and the island
that wasn't

Of all the monsters in the world there is none so fierce or so terrible as the Kraken. A Kraken is the size of an island; it can eat large ships in a single gulp and when it lashes its tail, whole cities on the shore will be flooded. If you just say the name "Kraken" to the bravest sailor with the biggest muscles and the largest anchor tattooed on his chest he will probably faint from fright.

The Kraken I am going to tell you about was, for many years, as terrible as any. He would eat a galleon for breakfast, a man-of-war for lunch, a pirate ship for supper and still sometimes gulp down a rowing boat for tea. But one day he didn't want to go on like this any more. The oars and sails that he swallowed were beginning to scratch the insides of his stomach and the screams of the sailors as he sucked them into his mouth gave him earache and made him feel depressed.

So he gorged himself on seaweed three times a day instead, which kept him perfectly healthy.

At the same time he decided to settle down because it is difficult to make friends if you are always roaring about flooding things and swallowing them.

The place he chose to settle down in was a peaceful, sunny bay with clear, deep water. The Kraken kept his neck and his huge, whiskery head with its big eyes, long eyelashes and intelligent forehead well down in the water and he kept his tail, which was scaly and interesting, in the water also, but he left his round, smooth back sticking out above the surface of the waves.

"Soon he began to make friends. His head made friends with a mermaid who lived in a grotto not far from his chin. She was no longer young and the songs she sang were rude because she had learned them from some sailors in a pub. This had happened when she came out on dry land for a while and married an innkeeper who had forced her to work as a barmaid.

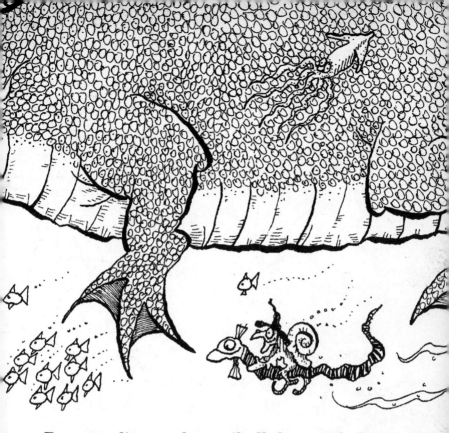

But standing on her tail all day made her
tired and when her husband said she
smelled fishy she had left him and
returned to the water. She was a
motherly mermaid and very fond of the
Kraken and he of her. The Kraken also
liked a rather dotty sea-witch who roared
about muttering spells like "Sweery,
sweery linkumloo", and usually ended

with someone being turned into a sea cucumber. And he liked the sea horses and the peacefully squelching squids.

The Kraken's tail, which was about half a mile away from it's head, didn't exactly make friends but the sea creatures made friends with it. Giant eels curled themselves round it and all those magic people that you find under the water – people whose front ends are horses and back ends are people, or whose back ends are fish and front ends are seals – used to swing on it and have fun.

With so many friends to talk to and seaweed to eat, the Kraken was very happy. But because its head was so busy at one end and it's tail so useful at the other, the Kraken forgot about its back, which was sticking hugely and humpily out of the water. And of course you will guess what happened next.

After about fifty years, grass seeds began to sprout on the Kraken's back and a meadow grew up, and among the grass the prettiest flowers – sea pinks and king-cups and forget-me-nots. Then a little larch tree managed to grow and another and another . . . and in the trees birds began to nest and to sing and to lay little, speckled eggs.

In short, the Kraken became the most beautiful and peaceful island you can imagine!

Naturally it was not long before people started rowing out from the village on the shore of the bay for picnics.

The Kraken did not mind this. The people who came were sensible and well behaved and would not have dreamed of leaving paper and broken glass about, and all that the Kraken could feel as they walked about on him was a very gentle tickle which was not at all disagreeable.

Then one day a large boat rowed out to the island and in it were five ordinary, nice little girls in clean pinafores with excited, shining eyes and five ordinary, sensible little boys in clean sailor suits with scrubbed and happy faces. These were the children of the village school on their Sunday Outing.

Also in the boat was the children's teacher who was called Miss Pigg but was not at all like a pig but very kind, Miss Pigg's mother, who was ninety-three, and two strong fishermen to do the rowing.

And if these had been the only people in the boat everything would have been all right but they were not. There was also a truly awful boy called Algernon.

It is quite possible that there has never been a child as unpleasant as this boy. Algernon lied and cheated. He kicked and bullied. When Miss Pigg tried to teach him to read he yawned or dribbled or fell off his stool and when he saw a stray kitten or puppy in the school yard he pelted it with stones.

But Algeronon, too, was at the village school so he could not be left out of the outing. The boat landed. Miss Pigg's old mother was placed on a tussock with her parasol open against the sun. Miss Pigg began to butter the sandwiches. And five sensible little boys and five well-behaved little girls ran about, so happy they thought they would burst. They took off their shoes and they paddled. They made daisy chains. They crawled through the grass pretending to be Ferocious Animals.

But not Algernon. Algernon was bored. He kicked the stones about and hit one of the little boys on the forehead. He pulled down a thrush's nest and trampled on the eggs. He found a little girl with her apron full of cowrie shells and threw them on the ground.

"I'm bored," he moaned. "There's nothing to do on this island."

But after lunch, when everyone was

resting, he did find something to do. He thought of it because it was the one thing Miss Pigg had told the children not to do on the island.

"You must not light a fire, children," she had said, "because it is dangerous and will damage the plants and trees."

And the five little girls and the five little boys had listened and nodded their heads. But not Algernon.

He gathered some sticks and he piled up some dry grass right in the middle and humpiest bit of the island. Then he crept to where one of the fishermen was sleeping and stole his matches. And then . . . he lit a fire!

The fire started small. But soon it caught a gust of wind and it grew and it spread.

At first the Kraken felt nothing at all. Then it felt a rather a strong tickle . . . then an itch . . . and then a pain!

"Ow!" said the Kraken, feeling very much upset.

Well, you will see what happened next and it is no use at all blaming the Kraken. If someone lit a fire on you, what would you do?

The Kraken sank.

He sank very slowly, because he was a monster who did not do things in a hurry, but he sank. And on the island the children saw the water rise over the fringe of sand, on to the grass, and up and up and into the button boots of Miss Pigg's mother sitting underneath the parasol . . .

"To the boats, children! Quick! Quick!" cried Miss Pigg.

She gathered up the smallest of the little girls and the smallest of the little boys and, with the rest of the children following her, she ran to where the fishermen were waiting in the boat.

Miss Pigg's mother, who was too old to run, climbed into her upturned parasol and floated towards the boat where the fishermen hauled her to safety.

But Algernon was still in the middle of the island, shouting and hooting around the fire.

"Algernon!" shouted Miss Pigg, standing up in the boat and waving her arms. "Algernon, come quickly!"

Too late! The island – and the boy – had gone!

Down and down went awful Algernon, down into the icy water . . . down and down he sank until he was level with the Kraken's gaping mouth.

The Kraken had of course meant to swallow Algernon, but when he saw the soggy, pulpy boy, he said: "I find I do not want to eat this child."

"Can't say I blame you," said the mermaid. "I wouldn't fancy him myself.

But what's to be done with him? They don't last more than a few minutes under water and we don't want dead bodies littering up the place."

"Perhaps the sea-witch could turn him into something?" suggested the Kraken.

"Good idea," said the mermaid. "I'll get her." And she swam off very quickly because Algernon was fast becoming waterlogged and magic does not work on people who are dead.

So the sea-witch came and did her spell, the one that began "Sweery, sweery linkumloo," and she turned Algernon into the thing he most reminded her of, which was a sea slug with a slimy body and blotchy spots.

As for the children and Miss Pigg and Miss Pigg's mother and the fishermen in the village, they were at first upset at losing their beautiful island. But when they realised that it had been a Kraken they became very excited. Soon people came from all over the world and gave the fishermen a lot of money to row them out to where the island had been. So the fishermen became rich and bought lovely clothes for their wives and children and were very happy. The Kraken, too, was happy because he had no more trouble with his back.

But whether Algernon was happy or not I cannot tell you. Some things are easy

and some things are difficult – and finding
out whether a sea slug is happy is very
difficult indeed!

the BOOBRIE and the SCOTSMEN WHO PRETENDED to BE SHEEP

Once upon a time three Scotsmen were walking through the Highlands on a cold winter's day when they came across some most unusual tracks in the snow. They were the tracks of webbed feet with curved claws on the end and each track was absolutely enormous, about the size of a house.

"Now what on earth can that be?" said Chief MacGregor, a tall, thin Scotsman with scars on his hairy knees from fighting in a battle.

"Whatever it is, it's mighty large," said Chief MacCallum, a small, fat Scotsman whose stomach bulged roundly beneath his kilt.

"We had better follow the tracks and see where they lead," said Chief MacDuff, an old, brave Scotsman who had lost a leg and painted his wooden one in the MacDuff colours of red, blue and green so that nobody would steal it.

So they followed the tracks of the webbed feet which looked as though whatever had made them was not only gigantic but also a bit knock-kneed and pigeon-toed because they pointed inwards. And when they had followed them for about an hour they came to a lake (only of course, being in Scotland, it was called a loch). At the edge of the loch there was the biggest nest they had ever seen, so big that it looked like one of those stockades made of logs that the settlers in America used to make to keep out Red Indians.

Inside the nest were three fluffy, round-eyed chicks with mottled feathers and yellow beaks. I do not mean anything sweet and little and quaint. These chicks were the size of full grown elephants, and as they jostled against each other and opened their huge beaks, the noise that came out was not "CHEEP!" but "BAA!"

The Scotsmen looked at each other and their knees began to tremble because they knew they had been following the tracks of the Boobrie bird and that these chicks were Boobrie chicks. They also knew that the chicks were saying "Baa!" instead of "Cheep!" because what Boobries feed on, mostly, is sheep.

"What are we going to do?" quavered tall, thin MacGregor

"The Boobrie will carry away all our livestock!" squeaked small fat MacCallum.

"We must make a plan," said brave MacDuff, striking his wooden leg with his walking stick.

So the Scotsmen walked back to their village and thought out what to do. They were quite right to be afraid. The Boobrie, which is a very Scottish bird, may not be very clever but it is so big that it seems to fill the whole sky when it appears and it is so strong that it can swoop down and carry off a sheep or a horse or a cow as easily as you could pick a daisy. A Boobrie's eyes are round and black and crazy looking, its beak is the size of a canoe and when it flies it makes a mournful, honking noise like a foghorn with stomach ache.

So the three Scotsmen thought and thought about what to do and then brave old MacDuff struck his forehead and said:

"I know! We will disguise ourselves as sheep and when the Boobrie swoops down on us we will shoot it with our horse pistols."

"And our blunderbusses!" yelled thin MacGregor.

"In its soft underbelly!" cried brave MacDuff.

Fat MacCallum didn't say anything because the idea of pretending to be a sheep and popping off bullets at the Boobrie made his poor underbelly quiver like a jelly. But he did not wish to seem a coward so all three Scotsmen began there and then to dress up as sheep.

This was difficult. First they had to find some sheepskins that fitted over their backs and then they had to go down on their hands and knees and see if they looked like sheep which mostly they didn't. MacDuff didn't because you don't often get sheep with wooden legs and

MacCallum didn't because he was so fat that he bulged out pinkly underneath like a sausage does when you fry it without pricking it first. And MacGregor certainly didn't because he had forgotten to take off his sporran and sheep with sporrans are very, very rare.

But in the end, by pulling and pushing at their skins and sticking extra bits of wool here and there they didn't look quite so bad and when they had practised saying "Baa" a few times they set off for the moor above the loch where they had first seen the Boobrie tracks.

They didn't like to walk upright carrying their sheepskins in case the Boobrie was watching, so they crawled and they had a very nasty time. Crawling in the snow is nasty anyway, and crawling in the snow while pretending to be a sheep and carrying a horse pistol, a blunderbuss and a catapult is even nastier. The Scotsmen fell and stumbled and their poor hairy legs, which weren't quite covered by the sheep hides, turned blue with cold. When they tried to say "Baa" their teeth rattled like doors in a high wind. But they crawled on till they reached the moor and then they huddled together and waited.

They did not wait for long.

The Boobrie did not come from the sky. It rose from the waters of the lake and the sight was one to turn the bravest man to stone. First came its head with its mad, round, staring eyes and then its terrible beak, curved like a pelican's to carry its prey, then its gigantic, feathered body rising like a living island from the water and lastly its webbed and house-sized feet.

It was the mother Boobrie. She was hungry and she was worried about her chicks and as she circled the moor, darkening the sky with her huge wings and making the mournful, honking noise that Boobries make, her crazy eyes searched anxiously for something to give them to eat. Round and round flew the Boobrie, searching and honking and presently the vast and worried bird saw exactly what she was looking for. Three sheep.

The Boobrie did not smile because birds don't but she was very pleased. One sheep would have been good, two would have been better, but three sheep – one for each of her chicks – was perfect. She circled once and dived down onto the moor.

This was the moment the Scotsmen had been waiting for. They had got it all planned. As the bird came down, they were going to step out from under their sheepskins, point their horse pistols, and their blunderbuss and their catapult at the soft underbelly of the bird – and fire!

What actually happened was different. As the Boobrie swooped down towards MacDuff, the brave Scotsman tried to lift his gun, got the catch wedged against his wooden leg and let loose a rain of bullets into a frozen cowpat.

Tall MacGregor managed to get his arm out and shoot off the blunderbuss but though he had filled it from a tin labelled Black Bullets these were not proper bullets but a dark kind of peppermint which has the same name - and if there is one thing you cannot kill a Boobrie with it is a rain of peppermints.

As for fat MacCallum, he had fainted clean away before he could loose his catapult with the brass bedknob which he had brought to fire at the Boobrie's heart.

The Boobrie, who was a bit short-sighted, did not notice any of these things. All she noticed were three ordinary, though rather wriggly, sheep.

So first she swooped down on brave MacDuff and picked him up and flew with him to the nest by the loch and dropped him down in front of Chick Number One.

Then she flew back and swooped down on skinny MacGregor and dropped him down in front of Chick Number Two. And lastly she went back for the MacCallum sheep which was a very quiet sheep, because the fat Scotsman was still in a faint.

After this the Boobrie felt very pleased with herself and waited for the chicks to start eating the sheep she had so kindly brought them.

But they didn't. The chicks looked down with their goofy pop-eyes at the sheep. They bent their scraggy necks. They pecked at the sheep with their webbed feet. And then they looked reproachfully at their mother.

"Not nice," said Chick Number One.

"Smells nasty," said Chick Number Two.

And Chick Number Three, who was the youngest, just said gloomily: "Legs." "Hairy," explained the first chick to its mother.

"Hairy legs."

"And wooden," said Chick Number Two, picking at the MacDuff sheep.

"Pink faces" said the youngest chick, who was taking it hard. He turned over the top end of the MacCallum sheep with its beak. "Horrid," it said, choking a little.

An anxious look spread over the mother Boobrie's face. She peered down at the nest, turned over MacDuff and lifted the sheepskin off MacCallum who had come out of his faint and was making a lot of noises, none of which were "Baa!"

The chicks were right. These were not proper sheep. A mistake had been made. And when you have made a mistake there is only one thing to do: put it right.

So the mother Boobrie picked up MacDuff in his sheepskin, carried him high in her beak and dropped him with a splash into the loch.

Next she picked up the MacGregor sheep, carried him high and dropped him

into the loch.

Then she went back for the MacCallum sheep and dropped him into the loch too.

And then she went flapping away on her enormous wings to go and look for some proper sheep because a mother's work is never done.

As for the Scotsmen, they managed to

swim ashore and hobble home, one in his underpants, one in his vest to which a frozen frog had stuck, and one in nothing but a large leaf and for the rest of the year they had chilblains in places it would not be polite to mention. MacDuff's wooden leg was lost in the water and so were all the rest of their things, which serves them right for trying to trick a Boobrie bird. Boobries may be a little silly, but if you give them time they can always tell a Scotsman from a sheep.

the brollachan whose mother was a fuath

this is a story about a Brollachan.

You will now want to know what a Brollochan is and I will tell you. A Brollachan is a dark, splodgy, shapeless thing. It has two red eyes, an enormous mouth and absolutely nothing else whatsoever. A Brollachan has no bones and no stomach and no nose. It has no arms and no legs and no feet and no toes and therefore no toe-nails. And it has no hair. There is probably nothing with less hair than a Brollachan.

A Brollachan, then, is just a squashy and quite frightening blob which rolls about the place. But though it has no shape of its own a Brollachan can take on the shape of things that it meets. A Brollachan lying on a table, for example, might become table-shaped or a Brollachan looking at a round Dutch cheese could become cheese-shaped if it wished. And though it cannot really think it can hear a little through its bulges and

76

it can certainly feel.

The Brollachan that this story is about lived in a house beside a swampy pond with his mother who was a Fuath. Fuaths are evil and bad-tempered fairies who live near water, so they are often dripping wet. They look almost like ordinary ladies, but if you look at them carefully you will find that there is something odd about them. Sometimes they are hollow from behind, and sometimes they have only one nostril.

The Brollachan's mother had a long nose with a black wart on it, whiskery ears, one frightful long tooth and webbed feet. She was a worrier and she was a nagger. She wanted the Brollachan to be more scary and more shapeless than he was. She wanted him to lure people into the swamp by terrifying them with his vile red eyes. She wanted him to bubble disgustingly in the mud at the bottom of the pond and she wanted him to speak.

"Say 'Mummy'," she would yell at him, "go on, say it. Say 'Mummy'."

But the Brollachan couldn't say anything. His mouth was big, but he used it for eating, not talking. So he would roll away sadly and suck in a large turnip or a dead rat or a ham bone and you would see them – the turnip or the rat or the ham bone – lying inside him sort of glowing a little until they gradually became part of the Brollachan because that is what

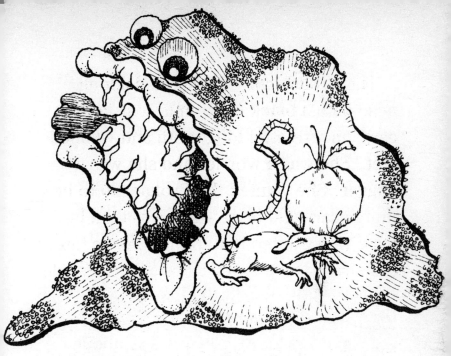

happens to the things that Brollachans eat.

All day long the Brollachan's mother followed him about flapping a wet cloth at the furniture and dripping water on him.

"I don't know what will become of you, Brollachan. Why aren't you outside drowning someone? Why are you sitting in that bucket? Why don't you do something with your life? And why don't you say 'Mummy'?"

79

The Brollachan tried hard to please her. But however wide he opened his mouth, all that came out was a kind of gulp or a sort of glucking noise.

Sometimes the Brollachan's mother invited her friends round; ladies like Black Annis who was a cannibal witch with a blue face or the Hag of the Dribble who was covered all over in grey slime, and then she would start:

"You don't know how I worry about him," she would say to these ladies, prodding the Brollachan with her webbed foot as he lay politely on the floor. "I can't sleep for worrying about him. He's so backward; he doesn't even try to frighten people into firs.

And he won't say 'Mummy'!"

"You should punish him," said the cannibal witch, burping rudely because she always swallowed people whole and this gave her wind. "Make him kneel on dried peas – nothing more painful than that!"

Which was not only cruel but a silly thing to say since the Brollachan did not have any knees.

One day the Brollachan and his mother went for a walk in the forest. The Brollachan liked the forest very much. It was not wet like the swamp where he lived and the leaves felt pleasantly tickly under his body. He stretched himself out more and more and became bush-shaped, then tree-shaped and then just Brollachan-shaped but extra large. He felt happy and he felt free.

But the Brollachan's mother was still talking. "Why don't you learn the names of the trees, Brollachan?" she said. "Why don't you at least try to give off an evil mist? There's a Brollachan in the next valley who has a whole village gibbering with fright every time he shows himself. And he can say "Mummy!"

After a while the Brollachan rolled away between the trees and he rolled and he rolled and he rolled until he was quite a way from his mother.

The Brollachan's mother did not notice this at first because she was too busy talking. "It's all right for you," she said, "you can't have a stomach ache from worrying because you haven't got a stomach. You can't have a headache from worrying because you haven't got a head.

You can't – Brollachan where are you?
Brollachan come here at once, I'm talking
to you. How dare you hide from your
mother! I can see your vile little red eyes
behind that tree. I know you're just

pretending to be that smelly toadstool.
Now come to your Mummy, Brollachan;
come at once!"

But the Brollachan was a long, long,
way away and he was well and truly lost.
He rolled on, however, until he came to
a little wooden house in a clearing and
because he was very tired by now, he
oozed through the crack under the door
and went inside.

It was a very nice house. There was
a fire in the grate and a painted stool and
a rocking chair in one corner. In the

rocking chair, fast asleep, sat an old man
with a kind face and a long white beard.
Everything was quiet and everything was
dry and the Brollachan liked it very much.
And becoming more or less the shape of
the hearthrug he lay down by the fire,
closed his vile red eyes and fell asleep.

He slept for one hour and he slept for
two while outside in the forest his mother,
the Fuath, roared about on her webbed
feet, searching and scolding and calling
him. Goodness knows how long he might

have gone on sleeping but just then a burning coal fell out of the fireplace and landed on one of the Brollachan's bulges.

Now the Brollachan couldn't talk but he could scream – and scream he did!

Everything then happened at once. The old man woke, saw that there was a Brollachan on his hearthrug and jumped from his rocking chair. The Brollachan's mother heard the scream and rushed in at the front door, dripping and shouting as she came.

"What's happened to you, Brollachan? How did you get here? Who hurt you? Has that nasty old man hurt you? Have you hurt my Brollachan, you stupid old man? Because if you have I'll turn you into

a bat with bunions. I'll turn you into an eel with earache. I'll claw you into strips of roast beef, I'll make newts come out of your nostrils, I'll . . ."

On and on she raged. The old man did not know how to bear so much noise. He took his long white beard and stuffed the left half into his left ear and the right half into his right ear but he could still hear the Fuath's voice. Feeling quite desperate he got a broom and tried to shoo

86

the Fuath out of doors.

But the Fuath would not be shushed and she would not be shooed. She just dripped and she threatened and she talked.

The Brollachan by now was quite upset. His burn did not hurt any longer but he felt that things were not as they should be. His red eyes were wide with worry and his shapeless darkness shivered at all this unpleasantness. What he wanted to do more than anything was to make things all right.

So he made himself very big and he opened his mouth and he went right up to his mother, who was still talking and scolding and waving her arms. If only he could do it! If only he could do the thing she wanted so much! Wider he opened his mouth and wider . . . and closer he went to his mother and closer . . . and harder he tried and harder . . . harder than he had ever tried in his whole life.

And then at last he did it. He actually did it!

"MUMMY!" said the Brollachan. "MUM – gluck – gulp!"

Then he stopped. His mother was not there.

The Brollachan was puzzled. He looked under the stool and behind the door, but there was no sign of her. But though he was puzzled, he was not worried. He felt very close to his mother. And because it made him tired to be so clever he lay down again – but further from the fire – and fell asleep.

The old man took half his beard out of his right ear and half his beard out of his left ear and came over to have a look. He could see the Brollachan's mother inside the Brollachan as clear as clear. He could even see the wart on the end of her nose. She was still talking and talking and

talking but Brollachans are soundproof so
he couldn't hear a thing.

So he smiled and nodded at the brolley
as if to say yes, you can stay, and went
back to his rocking chair.

The next day he made a fireguard so that the Brollachan would not get burnt. And he and the Brollachan lived together very happily. Because both of them had said all they were ever going to say and each was happy to let the other be the kind of person that he was.